Eugene Joseph Vincent Huiginn

Duxbury Beach

And other Poems

Eugene Joseph Vincent Huiginn

Duxbury Beach
And other Poems

ISBN/EAN: 9783743364929

Manufactured in Europe, USA, Canada, Australia, Japa

Cover: Foto ©Andreas Hilbeck / pixelio.de

Manufactured and distributed by brebook publishing software
(www.brebook.com)

Eugene Joseph Vincent Huiginn

Duxbury Beach

DUXBURY BEACH

AND

OTHER POEMS.

BY

E. J. V. HUIGINN.

BOSTON.

DAMRELL & UPHAM.

The Old Corner Bookstore,

283 Washington Street.

1894.

DEDICATION.

Pleased with myself? Why, no — I'm restless and
   feverish still,
    Longing to write a line that will live when I'm
      away,
A line that will help even one — aye the least — to
   know God's will
    And his deathless love and his Father's heart and
      his gentle sway.
No, I have no conceit that the lines which now I
   bring
    Are worthy to live, or worthy of him — just a drop
      in an endless sea—
But a friend or two will be pleased, how badly soe'er
   I sing,
    And to them I bring my song and they'll listen for
      love of me.

CONTENTS.

DUXBURY BEACH.

On that long beach that woos the Pilgrim sea
And guards the Pilgrim land from northern gales
We wandered at our will one Summer day,
And talked of earth and sea and heaven and God,
And read deep lessons into everything,
The grain of sand that lay upon the beach,
The pebble which had grown to larger life,
The shingly beach built up of drops of sand
That held the drop-made sea in its embrace
And murmured softly as in words of love,
While sea and sand each other chased in glee
All up and down the edges of the world,
And as a weed was tossed upon the shore,
Or singing shell was carried to our feet,
A silent joy through all our beings ran
To witness God's new wonders from the deep.
The sun and wind played gladly with the waves
And romped o'er hill and dale with bounding steps
That laughed with music in the ears of heaven.
We wondered at it all, the happy sea,

That imaged in its depths the bright blue sky,
The merry sand that sported with the waves,
The dancing breeze that rippled in its play
The smiling deep, the glorious sun that ruled
O'er all in majesty and love. Our souls
Reached forth and speeding far and wide beheld
The beauty of the home of God.

                        Spell-bound
We sat in silence in the shade of what
Was once a schooner though a ruin now :
It lay upon the ocean's verge a battered wreck,
All-blackened with the fire that wrought its doom.
With twisted bolts and sea-washed oaken pegs
Protruding from its every joint. The spray
Of fifty years had fallen on the keel
Which looked to heaven. Its history was unknown.
'T was found one morning on the wave-swept shore,
Dismantled, broken, ruined by the storm
Which lashed the wild Atlantic from the east
The previous night. What kindly hearts were lost
No one could tell. In some far-distant home
A mother, sister, wife, or sweetheart, wept
Its absence, longing with dull hopeless hope
For news of its return. Alas its fate
Was never heard! The orphaned baby lived
And grew a man of whitened locks, but still

No tidings heard he of his father's ship.
And now it lay upon the long white beach
Exposed to sun and storm, and from the storm
And sun affording shelter to the few
Who sought protection in its shade as there
It lay fast-anchored in a sea of sand.
    We felt the pathos of its life and spoke
Of human life, an echo of its own,
Its ups and downs, its joys and woes, and all
The mystery of being. It had its days
Of gladness as it sailed before the breeze
Upborne by the mighty sea, and, dipping,
Plunged on its way and bounded through the foam,
Which, dashing brightly, cheered the skipper's heart,
Who whistled as he hurried through the deep,
Or shouted forth a song as on he fled.
Again with shortened sail it bravely fought
The tempest in its fury as it swept
And howled with rage about the little bark
With creak and groan and straining of the mast.
For life it fought and won.—May God be praised!
    Such was its life. To-day lashed by the sea
Which yawns beneath its trembling keel
    and longs
To draw it to its death while wind and wave
Sing loud their boisterous song. To-morrow all

Is changed again, and no earth's mother's arms
Could twine about her child with truer love
Than the great deep's about the little craft.
But though we all escape from divers foes,
At last each thing of size and shape must die,
For so 'tis written in eternal law,
An end there is appointed unto each,
And little recks it when, or where, or how,
So we be ready for the newer life.
A fatal fire more dreadful than the sea
Attacked the schooner and with rushing flame
Destroyed its life.   Ah, God! the sea is Thine,
And in that hour of terror on the deep
Thou cared'st for Thine own while from their hearts
Poured forth the tide of love and trust in Thee
In the old hymn by sainted Wesley sung.
For in the dark a wandering vessel heard
The sound of voices rising on the wind.
While in the distance lay a smouldering fire
Upon the heaving bosom of the sea,
Which now began to answer to the storm
That shrieking through the sails called loud from
                              heaven.
The sweetest, saddest of all earthly songs
Was that last song of sailors as they felt
Their time had come to put into the port

Where Jesus takes the weary to his breast :—

> "Jesus, Lover of my soul,
>   Let me to Thy bosom fly,
> While the nearer waters roll,
>   While the tempest still is high :
> Hide me, O my Saviour, hide,
>   Till the storm of life is past :
> Safe into the haven guide ;
>   O receive my soul at last."—

It rose, and fell, and died upon the air,
Nor any song by earthly voices sung
More sweetly, sadly sounded in the world.
Next day the wreck was found upon the coast
Where we that morning sat beneath its shade
And drew life's lesson from its silent speech.
'T was thus we spoke of life : our earnest thoughts
At times subdued us as our glistening eyes
Sought sand and sea and sky and looked away.
Nor dared to look in one another's face.
Ah who can tell the great unspoken thoughts
That then possess the trembling soul of man
When sacred stillness reigns with feeling deep
And God alone and Nature hear him speak !
At length the wisest of us all began,
A man grown gray with wisdom's painful lore
Through sad experience gained in many lands :—

'This blackened wreck has taught us well to-day :
God's messenger it is and bravely speaks
Its message to us all. In joy and woe
Man's life is lived ; he too is but a ship
That carries in its hold the things of God
And meets with buffets sailing for the port.
All things we see are preachers unto him
Who wisely holds that Love has shaped the world,
And Love at length its purpose must fulfil.
I have been tossed, as was this ship, on seas
That stunned my soul and drove me up a wreck
Upon the wastes that border earth and hell.
False friends and sin and sorrow, at their will,
In fury rushed upon me and in glee
Made wreckage of my faith and love for God :
This earth was hell, and life a curse : I cried
Aloud—There is no God, not one, no, no :
Not one who cares for us who call to him
As Father Everlasting, Boundless Love :
No God, but demons who contrive to bring
Swift desolation to the sons of men,
And loudly scream ha, ha, in mocking tones !
Their shouts of triumph maddened all my being
And rising in the face of God I yelled
Defiance to his throne, and fainting fell
Abandoned, ruined, on the heedless earth.

Men talk of torments from the hand of God,
Or from those spirits fell which they create,
God's vengeful lictors of unwept-for sins—
But man is man's worst demon, and the worst
Of all man's conscience to himself. I speak
From life's great lesson unto me. In hate
I crushed out God, but sin could bring no rest
To my o'ertortured soul.

              'Twas then that one—
Who thinks forever in her inmost life
Of one she lost, a mother's grandest hope.
Long years before when falling from a height
His noble life from earth passed up to God,
Since when she lives with God and him in heaven—
O'erheard my cry of anger and of pain,
And feeling for my wretched, godless state
Spoke words of comfort and of peace to me
While pitying tears rolled from her gentle eyes.
O blame me not that I had cast aside
All faith in God and man! My life was led
In wicked ways from youth. No mother's love
Had sent great prayers to God for her dear child—
Perhaps she prayed in that God's greater world,
But I no prayer from spirits blest could hear.
No father's care had guided me to right,
And taught me that in virtue I must seek

Life's purpose, as all life from virtue springs.
    I was the dupe and plaything of the world :
A grasping cousin seized the good estate,
Which he, as guardian, from my father held,
And cast me out upon the city's life.
While he, false traitor to a dead man's faith,
And falser to a dead man's helpless child,
Drank deeper draughts to drown his sickening guilt.
Despising all and hating all I met
My soul still clamored for its truer life,
For sin can never from the soul efface
All memory of its birth from Life all-pure.
But all things reeked of blasphemy and sin :
The priest who swung his censer in the church,
And scented the foul air to please high heaven
And hold his little sway o'er savage minds—
Who bartered for a price the blood of God—
From out the brass, or gold, or silver, sent
A clouding fume for his own stenchful lusts.
The men who posed for statecraft in the world,
The proud-faced dames who trampled on the poor,
The cheat and swindler in the city's marts,
The scandal-mongers of the daily press,
The rogues who swaggered in the city's streets—
Pretended guardians of the rights of men,
The judges who protected justice well

By keeping her enveiled from human sight,
The very children at their mothers' breasts!—
All, all, were laughing at the face of Christ.
To me there was no goodness in the world :
The gilded dens of infamy and vice,
Where Lust sits crowned and Wantonness adores.
Shamed homes where so-called honest maidens rushed
To lecherous arms in mockery of love
And sacred purity of marriage bliss :
The one received her price a slave to none,
The other for her price a slave became.
There was no God : no God to me, no Christ.
　　To wicked men all goodness is a lie,
And I had grown to hate the thought of good
Which nowhere could I find.
'Twas then that she,
The holy mother of a godlike boy,
With tears and prayers became a Christ to me,
A very Jesus to a sinful man,
And led me back to God from whom I came,
And showed me all the beauty of the world,
And taught me all the graciousness of truth.
In her I found my God, and when I stand
All-purified from sin before his face
I'll take her hand and lead her to the throne,
And tell my Father of her love to me,

And ask him to outpour his bounding life
In countless blessings on her holy head.

    Since then I've walked upon the blessed earth
And found the mystery of joy and woe
In man's submission to the highest will.
In patience and in peace I wait for him
To tell me more when he shall call me home.
Earth, sea, and sky, proclaim the law of life,
Which teaches us through all there is no death.
From this poor wreck we wisdom learn
    while here
We sit beneath its shade. That sea too tells
Its message to us all. Upon its breast
It bears the commerce of the world from land
To land ; it gives its treasures to support
Man's life and beautify his home and him :
Its cooling pity tames the fierce hot sun,
And in ten thousand ways it blesses life.
Again, in anger it upshrieks to heaven
And catching in its grasp the mighty ship
With dire destruction dashes on the shore
And fringes all the earth with death and foam.
While rending cries from stricken hearts uprise.
Such is its endless life, a friend, a foe ;
In peace, in wrath,—like men in grace and sin—
Though men are subject unto grace alone.

But freely of themselves submit to sin."
A gentle sadness swept us while he spoke,
And gratitude to God possessed our hearts
That Virtue yet can master in the world.
The scorners still will scorn what men call truth,
And mock at goodness as a thing of choice,
A name to please the fancy of the weak,
To cozen souls and cheat them out of peace,
By cunning men suggested in the past.
But we who heard the lapping of the sea
On that long beach and listened to the voice
Of him who spoke and told us of his life
Of sin and wrong and ruinous despair,
And of God's goodness wrestling with it all,
Felt as if God were speaking from the deeps
The only real in this changing world.

    The youngest of us all in years a child,
But sweetened with the wisdom childhood brings
From out its native home, God's deepest love,
Then drew a circle in the soft white sand,
And said, "So is God's love as is God's life,
Without beginning as without an end,
Encircling all and waiting in the calm
Of his great being for the purposed will,
When virtue only shall survive in all,
And all the memory of sin be gone :

Our God will wait, in patience still will wait,
His love is deathless as his endless life."

    I often wander on that Pilgrim strand,
And watch the silent ebbing of the sea,
And see the Mayflower sweeping into port,
And hear the Pilgrims sing their hymns of praise,
But oftener still I linger by that wreck,
And hear our voices as we spoke that day,
And his, the strong man's, telling of his life,
And hers, the maiden's, telling us of God,
And God's in all, and always I exclaim,
"His love is deathless as his endless life."

REVERIES.

Brave Saviour of the human race,
　Lo, we—who were not there to see
　Still Hermon's wondrous mystery,
Thy glowing and transformed face :

Nor saw the Prophets at Thy side,
　Nor heard the voice from out the cloud,
　"This is my son, hear him,"—nor bowed
Our faces low our fears to hide—

Come, Christ, to Thee, Thou Light Divine.
　Thou knowest all we are to be,
　Mere nothingness bereft of Thee,
We come to Thee for we are Thine.

Thou knewest us before our birth,
　To Thee the darkness is as light.
　All things are open to thy sight,
Who madest all the heavens and earth.

That settest all the bounds of time,
　And things that were not mad'st to be
　Reflections of Thy majesty
And destined unto ends sublime.

Thy wisdom and Thy wondrous power
   Are seen in all around, above,
   Thy watchful care, Thy deathless love,
Sustaining all from hour to hour:

From hour to hour, and here and there,
   Thy presence is in all revealed,
   For all things with Thy seal are sealed
And own Thy lordship everywhere.

Lo, we, Thy creatures, come to Thee,
   For Thou our weary earth hast trod,
   And interlinked our souls with God,
And shown us what we are to be,

And how the battle must be fought,
   And helpest in the deadly strife,
   For Thou art still the Bread of Life
That givest strength to souls Thou'st bought.

We know in whom we have believed,
   Howe'er the sceptic scoff and sneer,
   Despite the unbeliever's jeer,
Who trusts in Thee is not deceived.

Thou art the Saviour of our faith,
   And at Thy name all nations bow,
   And cry for help as we do now,
O lift us from the gates of death!

We fail before our work is done,
  We faint and falter day by day,
  Our souls are weak and oft we say,
"I am but one! I am but one!"

But one and frail, nor can I know
  The things ordained of Thee to be
  In time, nor in eternity,
Nor into what myself may grow.

In life, in death, in woe, in weal,
  O who can tell Thy deep design,
  Or why the suns so brightly shine,
Or if things inorganic feel?

We can but know if Thou wilt tell,
  For Thou alone hast come from God,
  And in the flesh the earth hast trod,
And taught us how in faith to dwell:

In faith like her who kissed Thy feet,
  And wiped them with her flowing hair,
  And prayed to Thee in her despair,
And grew in grace and love complete.

Like her, I come to thee to-night,
  For all my soul is steeped in pain,
  O let my cry be not in vain,
Lord, save me by Thy gracious might!

Alone with none but God to hear,
  In deep dark stillness all alone,
  I weep for that departed one,
Who died with the expiring year.

My soul in anguish lives again
  Beside that dying one who vowed,
  Though wrapped up in his graveyard shroud,
To guide me through the wiles of men.

He comes to me as once before,
  He stands beside me in the room,
  And thick and dark though be the gloom,
I know 'tis he that comes once more.

He grasps my hand with loving grasp,
  He kisses me upon the face,
  He holds me in a close embrace,
As oft he did in loving clasp.

He speaks as spirits only speak,
  He calls to mind my youth again,
  I sob in anguish wild, and then
His lips he presses on my cheek.

He brings a message o'er the sea,
  His voice with deepest anguish thrills,
  And darkest grief my bosom fills,
My heart is rent with misery.

The years are slowly speeding on
  Since he was laid within the tomb.
  My life is all enwrapped in gloom,
And death comes claiming one by one.

My lips drew in his latest breath.
  I heard the latest gurgling roll,
  I prayed with all my strength of soul,
And held him as he slept in death.

The room was filled with sobbing prayers,
  I wept upon his pallid face,
  And clasped him in a close embrace,—
Death came for him so unawares!

The loving, tender voice was still,
  The lover, husband, father, gone,
  His soul was at the Judge's throne,
His body limp in death and chill.

Beside his whitening corpse I stood,
  My father's corpse—I stood aghast!
  The King had claimed his own at last,
The noblest of our race and blood.

My eyes were fixed upon his face,
  I wondered where his life had fled,
  I thought on all the good priest said
Of other worlds and Jesus' grace.

A silence lay upon the hall.
   A deep dark woe upon it hung.
   A pall of grief was round it flung.
Death brought an anguish to us all.

We followed to the place of rest.
   And laid him with the silent dead.
   We prayed above his lowly bed,
And cast the clay upon his breast.

The priest in sobbing anguish sang :—
   "O God, Thy grieving ones sustain !
   Who comes to Thee shall live again."—
And all the air with sorrow rang.—

"Who comes to Thee, Eternal Son.
   In faith, though dead, shall never die.
   O hear our broken-hearted cry !
Thy will be done !   Thy will be done !"

Beside the church we laid him low.
   The cross we fixed upon his grave.
   The emblem that alone can save.
And God enveloped all in snow.

O buried deep in churchyard mould !
   O Father, can you hear my pain?
   Come to me, clasp me once again,
Your heart though dead cannot be cold !

How silent is the stillness round !
    Who gave me breath no more will hear :
    My life is now so sad and drear.
I long to hear the Trumpet's sound.

To-night it all comes back to me,
    For I have heard one from the tomb,
    He stood beside me in the gloom,
And I am filled with agony.

He came before when mother died,
    He stayed with me through all the time
    Until the death-watch tolled the chime,
And then departed from my side.

Not twice the earth did gird the sun
    From father's death till in the night
    That father's spirit wan and white
Told me my mother's race was run.

She blessed me in her latest breath,
    Her dying eyes were lit with love,
    She smiled as if at God above,
And calmly yielded her to death.

In shrouds she lay upon the bed,
  They wept for me her only child,
  Her face in death upon me smiled.
She seemed to think and feel though dead.

Again the hearse with nodding plumes
  We followed to the graveyard old,
  Again we cast the churchyard mould
Upon the coffin mid the tombs.

Her kind old pastor took his place,
  And cast the clay that should be cast,
  And gave the blessing at the last,
And wept above her buried face.

My soul has sorrowed from that hour,
  I've prayed—oh! was it wrong to pray?
  That I might mingle with her clay,
And grow into the self-same flower.

The hopes of all my youth have fled,
  They've vanished from me one by one,
  The last, the best, has failed and gone.
I'd feel content if with the dead.

O Mother fairest of our race,
   The sweetest flower on all our tree,
   How can I now apart from thee
Live in this lonely, loveless place?

Away across the foamy sea
   Thou sleep'st beneath the churchyard sod,
   Thy face upturned in death to God,
And I no more can gaze on thee!

Can gaze on thee and tell the pain,
   The weary pain of all the years,—
   And mingle with my tale the tears
That start and flow repressed in vain,—

The deathly pain of human life,
   Where men contend for private gain,
   Where hatred, lust, and murder reign,
And all is brutal, savage strife ;

Where brutish beasts are juster far
   And kinder to their helpless young,
   That from their wombs and loins are sprung,
Although they preach no Avatar,

Than he who lords it o'er the earth,
   And calls himself creation's King,
   Whose praises all the poets sing,
With all his boasted second birth,

Is to his brother fellow-man
   With memory and will and mind.
   God's counterpart, by him designed
Like God in his eternal plan,—

And yet this weary earth was trod
   By him who taught that men were one,
   Co-members in the mystic Son,
Co-heirs with Christ, the Son of God!

Last night I sat in weary pain,
   My thoughts went wand'ring through the years,
   My eyes were wet with starting tears
For all the wilful ways of men.

And while I pondered in the gloom :—
   "Will man forever miss his end,
   And be himself his own worst friend,
Nor learn a lesson from the tomb.

"Nor catch the meaning of his life?"—
   I heard the tramp of crowding feet,
   And angry voices in the street,
And thronging men as if in strife.

And clang of sword, and trumpet sound,
  And ringing horse-hoofs passing by,
  And deadly hatred's fiercest cry,
And blasphemies the place confound,

And man in frenzy shriek to man
  In hatred's fiercest tones of hell,
  "If he be King of Israel,
Let him come down now."—So it ran.

And so it runs through all the time
  The unbelief of human minds,
  Who, tossed about by all the winds
Of doubt, become the dupes of crime.

And, rushing from the feet of God,
  Suspend him on the cross alone,
  And sin and passion high enthrone,
And deify the earthy clod.

And deeper grew my woe within,
  And louder came the human cry,
  "Away with him, the Christ must die!"
O keep me from a world of sin!

O hide me, Saviour of the race,
  From thoughts, that surge like thronging hosts,
  And haunt my mind like wand'ring ghosts,
Of Thy beloved and bleeding face!

O save me, Christ, some little faith,
  And bring me back, O Lord to Thee,
  I cannot ree life's mystery,
Nor read the secrets known to death.

We cannot see, our eyes are dim,
  The things that God alone can see,
  And yet in pride how often we
Reject the things we know of Him !

He gives us gifts beyond our ken,
  He prints his image on the clod,
  And, oh ! because we are not God,
We think we're more or less than men !

And each to each a liar is,
  And each his brother throttles down,
  And robs him of his fair renown,
And gold that he had thought was his :

And laughs at God, and right, and wrong,
  And scorns the altar, and the priest,
  And makes with sin a joyous feast,
And sings a loud triumphant song :

And holds the harlot to his heart,
  And presses kisses on her face,
  And scoffs at sacrament and grace,
And worships science, love, and art :

And fills the brimming glass with wine,
   And damns the God of all the creeds,
   The God, who hate and discord breeds,
And drinks to heavenly lust divine:

And points the way for man to rise
   From high to higher every age,
   Though bestial passions in him rage,
And claps his hands and "Forward!" cries.

Yes, forward! up the slopes of time,
   Along the plains of sin and care,
   And lustful love and grim despair,
And quickly down the steeps of crime!

Forgotten be the home, the wife,
   The babe upon the mother's knee,
   No claims of duty now can be.
He lives within the higher life.

The higher life! and he can tell,
   How he has cast the Christ aside,
   And all the ravings of his pride,
Confusions all of heaven and hell.

And Reason's flag he has unfurled,
   And shattered all the world of awe,
   And he has freed himself from law,
While placing law on all the world.

And he has burst the bonds of sin,
  His passions being his only lord.
  He has no fear, seeks no reward,
For he is close to God akin :

Aye, he is God ! he claims,—and he
  On other godheads wages war,
  For either things eternal are,
Or soon in nothingness shall be.

He cannot think when time began,
  Nor when 'twill end, nor space confine.
  And thus he argues line by line,
Eternal too must be the man :

And, reaching through eternal years,
  Dethrones the God who rules the world,
  And on his banner high unfurled
Inscribes, "There is no God," and cheers.

And so he drains the foaming bowl
  Of poisoned passion, pride, and lust,
  For "Earth to earth, and dust to dust,"
Bring no refining to his soul :

And laughs at all the fools of fear,
  And trains his child in unbelief,
  And seeks in every change relief,
And fights with God from year to year :

And, beaten, finds his infant son
　　Has found a God within his breast,
　　And weeping sore is deep distressed
Because his father is alone.

His child who, childlike, sadly weeps,
　　And prays in secret while he kneels
　　To him who truth to all reveals,
And calls to him from out the deeps :—

"O hear my cry, most Blessed Lord,
　　And bless my father with Thy light,
　　And guide his steps to Thee aright,
And teach him how to know Thy word :

"To know Thy word and live with Thee
　　Conjoined in love with all his kind,
　　And take the doubts from out his mind,
And make him with Thy freedom free :

"And bring him to the feet of Christ
　　In hope, as Thou alone dost know,
　　And make him with Thy faith to glow,
And with Thy love eternalized.

"To Thee, O God ! I pour my prayer,
　　And crave through Christ that Thou wilt save
　　My father from the deepening grave
Of unbelief and dark despair."

So prays he with his face in tears,
  And all his soul in striving pain—
  Who says such prayers are said in vain?
God is not swayed by bigots' sneers.

And when the shepherd's bell shall sound
  And all the sheep of God are told,
  Among the safe within the fold
That child and father will be found.

—

The snow lay deep upon the hills,
  The woodsmen plied their busy teams,
  And put the lumber in the streams,
Preparing for the shrieking mills.

I knelt within the forest church,
  'T was on the day the Saviour died,
  The churchyard trees in sorrow sighed,
The snow lay drifted at the porch :

The villagers in silence knelt,
  And joined in earnest, fervent prayer,
  A sadness deepened on the air,
And all a subtle presence felt.

—

I read the Gospel from Saint John,
　And told them of the thorny crown,
　And of the cross that crushed him down,
The broken-hearted friendless One.

I told them of the ruthless rood
　On which he died disdained, disgraced,
　The stamp of God in him defaced,
His face and form besmeared with blood.

And how he bowed in deep despair,
　And raised the agonizing cry,
　"My God! oh! why forsake me? why?"
And called to mind his dying prayer.

And, oh! the weight of human woe
　That pressed them as I tried to speak
　Forced tears to flow down every cheek
That spite of all would spring and flow:

Would spring and flow—I ceased to preach,
　A dreary sorrow swept my soul,
　A sorrow I could not control,
And thought refused to come in speech.

I knelt, and wept, and tried to pray,
　And then we sang the touching hymn,
　" 'T is finished"—and with eyes still dim
I blessed them ere they went away.

O ye who laugh at simple faith
    And Christ, who died to make men good,
    Who yet proclaim man's brotherhood,
Why hunt again the Christ to death?

O tell me what the Saviour's crime?
    He conquered all the powers of hell,
    And taught all men in love to dwell,
God's children all in every clime:

He preached forbearance to the race :—
    "Forgive and ye shall be forgiven,
    And live in blessedness in heaven
With God forever face to face."

And prayed in tenderness and ruth :—
    "O fill them with Thy love divine,
    For mine are Thine, and Thine are mine,
And sanctify them with Thy truth!

"My Father! now the hour is come,
    Unite them all in love to Thee,
    As I in Thee and Thou in me,
And guide them to Thy heavenly home!"

O ye who scorn the Son of Man,
    Consumed in self-conceit and pride,
    Who curse the lowly Crucified,
And laugh at all Redemption's plan,

Wherein has Christ mankind oppressed?
  Or scorned the lowly or the poor?
  Or sent the beggar from his door
With empty hand or aching breast?

He died to make the nations free,
  He stretches out a loving hand,
  He pours his grace on every land
From shore to shore, from sea to sea.

From sea to sea and everywhere,
  And not a life can live or die,
  And not a soul in anguish cry,
But he, the Saviour-Christ, is there.

I feel him in my inmost heart,
  As sitting in the silent room
  I watch the men repair the boom
Which swollen floods have sprung apart.

I felt him through the lonely night,
  As praying by death's lowly bed
  I saw a radiance overspread
The dying face, a mystic light—

A holy light that seemed to shine
  Round him who from a deep sea-grave
  His life had risked a life to save
And emulated love divine.

I knew he had no fear of loss,
   I saw him weep the other day
   As in the church he knelt to pray
And heard the story of the Cross.

And Christ was with him, for he spoke
   As talking to a present friend,
   And smilingly he met the end
And passed away as morning broke.

O ye of unbelieving minds
   Who war with all the jangling creeds,
   Who live in doubt and not in deeds,
Wherein has Christ oppressed mankind?

Sum up the guilt of all the years—
   The crimes of frenzied christian rage,
   The bloodshed, lust of every age,
And all the seas of scalding tears :

The priesthood of eternal hate,
   Who lighted up the seething fires,
   And cast the saints upon the pyres,
And damned them all as reprobate,

And preached a creed all blood-enstained,
  And made of earth a raging hell,
  And swung the censer, rang the bell,
And lived in riot unrestrained,

And ground the human race to dust,
  And hampered all the powers of mind,
  And tried to keep the nations blind,
And battened on the spoils of lust,

And grasping hard the flaming rod
  Of fury robbed the sons of men,
  And robed themselves in vestments then
To pacify an angry God!

And crushed to earth the starving poor,
  And trampled on the orphan's right,
  And stole the weeping widow's mite :—
Does Christ such crimes as these endure?

I cannot calm my rising grief,
  Nor chase the film that veils my eyes,
  Nor can I solve the doubts that rise,
Despite my strong and firm belief.

I wish to roam through endless space,
  And look upon the face of God,
  And ask him how the human clod
Is worth redemption, love, and grace :

And if the dead in deathless strife
  Contend with agonizing care,
  And want and woe and grim despair,
And weary of eternal life :

Or, freed from trammelings of dust,
  Crowd fiercely to the marts of crime,
  And worship sin with faith sublime,
Entangled in the toils of lust :

And if they're ranked in class and class,
  And buy the highest ranks with gold,
  And trace their kinship as of old,
And call the poor "the vulgar mass."

Do nations spill each other's blood,
  And race wage deadly war on race,
  Contending for the foremost place,
All-heedless of the voice of God?

Oh! if they live in such excess,
  If Christ has died without avail—
  My God! then let my being fail
And fall back into nothingness!

LONGINGS.

I wish that God would give me power to speak
  The thoughts that come and go of human life—
That life I feel in me, but words are weak
  And helpless to explain the deathless strife,
And how God's life immortal throbs in me
And folds me in its awful mystery.

'Tis only God of his own life can tell,
  And his infinitude of holiness,
Of his eternal love which can compel
  Our saddened hearts, uplifting in distress,
And making us the children of his love
More like himself his boundless care to prove.

We often yield before the tempter's smile,
  And please ourselves declaring our release
From law of God or soul, and for a while
  In our own ways we revel, but the peace
That crowns a life self-centred in its own
Is not the peace of man, God's gifted son.

O brothers, come, ascend the lofty height
 Where God, our Father, dwells in majesty.
Look deep into those eyes of love, the bright,
 Warm glance of infinite affection see,
And read the glorious meaning of their look!
God's eyes,—to us God's holy, open book!

O great pathetic wondrous eyes of God!
 In you I see all weakness overcome,
In you the calvaries that men have trod,
 Transformed with all the bounding joy of home,
In you I see all sorrows at an end,
Eyes of my God, my Father, and my Friend!

CREDO.

Yes, I am pleased with the world, though not quite in
    love with its sins ;

Its lust and its rapine are stains, but these were not
    fashioned in heaven.

'T is easier far to be bad than be good, for nature is
    bad

And man has corrupted himself and an heir of cor-
    ruption is born—

The ages in prayer and in chant, and in creed and in
    sermon have held.

That man is in natural sin, God-ordered at war with
    his God,

And loving the bad from his birth, a creature of
    whimsical wrath,

Bought out by a murderous deed from the wrath of a
    love without bounds—

No, no : such a creed is all false and unjust to the
    Giver of life !

The war is in man with himself as he fashions through
    instincts of right

His soul like his God, and stumbles and falls by the
    way,

For the task is immense and Godlike, and frail is the
    nature that strives,

My creed then is simple and strong, that God is the
    Ruler of all,

And never has cursed even one, not the sinfullest ever
    that lived,

But knows in his patience and might that love is the
    fountain of life,

And life must go back to its source because infinite
    love must prevail,

And God is the essence of love, and at last must be
    Lord over all.

TO MARTHA.

May gladness fill thy little heart,
And crown thy life in every part!
And wheresoe'er, dear child, thou art,
    God bless thee, little girl!

Be God-like as thou art to-day,
In truth, in holiness, alway:
And while I live for thee I'll pray—
    God bless thee, little girl!

If sorrow come thy joy to sting,
God's great warm love around thee cling!
God's holy spirits ever sing—
    God bless thee, little girl!

May life for thee be always sweet
As breath of God; thy loving feet
In his own paths; his smile e'er greet
    And bless thee, little girl!

CHRIST'S ANSWER.

Down-sloped the sun and wandered to the west
The afternoon of one bright summer day,
Within the church I watched his beams at play
Round Christ's crown-gloried head; my soul, o'erpressed
By the deep mystery of sin's dark blot,
Prayed the dear Saviour in the window-pane
That he to me the meaning would explain
Of life and sin and man's predestined lot.
The parted lips of Jesus softly spoke,
"God gives man power to prove his love for God
In woe and weakness as in strength :
                                    I trod
The wine-press all alone, and, dying, broke
Temptation's might and sorrow's. Ye must pray
And wait God's will in his revealing day."

TO VERNETTE.

Little sweet-heart of the Christ,
Baby dearest all unpriced,
    God again renews in thee
    All this wondrous world for me,
Sanctifying our sad earth
With the mystery of thy birth
    And with thy angelic face
    Brightening every darkened place.

Baby dearest, God's own bloom,
Thou dost drive away all gloom,
    Laughing, smiling, all day long
    Cooing God's undying song.
Flower of the eternal love,
Thou his deathless care dost prove
    From his own all-holy life
    Blessing all our earthly strife.

"Little Christ," whose tiny voice
Echoes God's while we rejoice,
    Beam of God, whose warming rays
    Fill our hearts with joyous praise,
Preach to us our Father's will
Conqu'ring every shape of ill,
    Make us all but him forget,
    Breath and bloom of God, Vernette!

MY CREED.

It was a happy day : the little birds
Did sweetly tune their carols on the breeze,
And fill the throbbing air with richest songs
In language taught them of their Father, God,
And in the music of their songs you felt
They sent their souls' deep adoration back
To the great fountain of their joyous being,
Who understood their every note of joy.
The mountain stream dashed merrily along
And roystered round the rocks with sportive love
And sprightly step and merry laughing face
That glowed with sunshine in the eyes of heaven
As on it bounded to the waiting sea.
The woods stood still in silence as in thought
Great souls in contemplation of their God.
All things suggested holiness and life,
And peace unbroken and unmeasured joy,
A fitting home for God and noble souls,
Where they might mingle in eternal love,
And each with each hold rapturous converse deep
In the mysteriousness of solitude.

With him alone I wandered through the woods
And opened all the longings of my heart
To him ; he saw me as I am, and he
Alone of all the world can understand
The weakness and the strength of my young life,
The desolation of my soul as sin
Triumphant carries me away from him,
The peace that waits for me on my return,
The aspirations that with heavenward flight
Tend always to their home ; the loves, the joys,
The sorrows, that control my daily being.
From him I hid no thought that ever marred
The holiness of his great gifts to me.
I told him how I loved his life in all
The world and hoped 'gainst hope that sanctity
And peace would reign supreme at length ;
                       that sin
And sorrow never could dethrone my faith
In the all-loving father of the world.
He spoke no word of stern rebuke to me
Although I dared to tell him on that day
That evil must be vanquished in the end
Despite what priest or preacher might declare,
Because his good would conquer through his love.
This faith he gave me in the glorious Christ.
And year by year as I approach to him

And try to read the secrets of the world
And all the height and depth of human life
My faith grows deeper, greater in that Christ.
God's Son, Revealer of the Father's will.

Oh, why will men usurp the place of God
And pass their judgments on their Father's sons!
Has life been vain? How often in the past
The priest has offered up the God-man's blood
Of blessing and a loud Te Deum sung
In gratitude to God for murderous deeds
Of men on men, God's children on themselves.
And turn by turn as human craft might win.
Or savage force o'er savage force prevail,
Made God and Jesus partners in their crimes.
And sprinkled God's own altars with the blood
Of Jesus, Son of Man and son of God!

How often has the preacher standing there
In broidered robe to lend him false repute
Before God's own poor weak and sinful men.
Consigned with awful imprecations souls
To torments endless and eternal hate,
As if he spoke for him the Prince of Peace.
The very angel of undying love!

In the deep solitude with God I thought
Of all the past, and daringly I told
My love and faith and hope, and he was pleased :

For from the woods the song-birds gathered round
And sang their creed of peace and trust and joy :
The river murmured with a gladder strain,
While through the trees the whisp'ring breezes passed
And on the branches played their sweetest songs.
　　And every day since then I walked with God
I feel my faith forever burst its bounds
And bring me more and more into that life,
My God's, for which his love created me.

THE WANDERING JEW.

An old man sat on the mountain peak
  And he gazed on the earth below,
And he shook his head with a gloomy shake,
With its hair as white as the bright snow-flake,
  Whilst his hands beat to and fro,
And the winds seemed hushed as he slowly spake.
  And told his tale of woe.

"My hair, O my son! is silver white,
  And my brow is ploughed with seams,
For sorrow and care have been my lot
Since years ago I was on this spot
  And thought of my boyhood's dreams,
Boy's dreams that vanished from out my sight
  As a mist in the day-god's beams.

"I had dreamt of a home where no care could be,
  Where joy and content should reign,
Where the peace of God should hold the place,
And all by his grace wear a happy face,
  Where none should e'er complain;
And, dreaming, such was the home I did see,
  But my dreaming all was vain.

"And to find such a place I left my home
Full of hope in my youthful breast,
But a mocking voice followed on from behind,
And a mocking laugh followed on on the wind,
And my heart was with grief oppressed,
And now by decree I am forced to roam
Till the world shall come to rest."

And the old man stopped in his tale and sighed
As he gazed on the earth and sky,
And the tears down his cheeks ran quick and fast,
And he seemed to be wrap'd in thoughts of the past,
Then he spoke with a weary sigh :—
"'Twas the day that Jesus was crucified,
And when on his way to die :

"I stood in the door as he staggered on,
And I joyed in the bloody deed,
And he wished to rest, for the weight of the cross
And the scourge and the crown had caused such a loss
Of his strength he for rest did plead,
But I pushed him away, the Eternal son !—
And scoffed at him in his need.

"And Jesus beneath the cross still bowed,
As he paused on his weary way,
Condemned me to wander away from home

And restless and friendless ever to roam,
   Nor rest till the judgment day :
And still I can hear the jeering crowd,
   And our Saviour my sentence say.

"And I've wearily roamed since that dreadful time
   And I'm whitened with age and care
But wherever I go I can see the Tree,
And Jesus nailed to it and dying for me,
   And I try to hunt despair,
For the memory of my terrible crime
   Is with me everywhere.

"And I pray that the judgment soon may come,
   And I long for the Trumpet's blast,
Till then I must wander the world alone,
And pray the Redeemer who died to atone
   To pardon my sin at last ;
And I hope with my Jesus to find a home
   When my wearisome life is past."

He spoke, and he left the mountain peak
   With fears and griefs oppressed,
And I thought I could hear a voice behind,
A voice that followed him on the wind,
   And bade the wanderer rest.
And I thought I could hear the Saviour speak
   And welcome him to his breast.

LOVE IN SORROW

Man cannot understand himself, and in
The anguish of his heart he turns to Thee,
His God, and claims Thee for his own.   The pain
Of life is seamed upon his face in lines
Of agony and grief and care which come
To all.   At night he dreams of love and joy,
And earliest dawn his happiness destroys :
He watches Death with secret silent step,
Or swift, or slow, come taking one by one
From out the circle of his love, and woe
In sombre darkness sits upon his soul,
And mourning in close-fitting robes of black
Stalks gloomily along and meets him face
To face.   At every turn his path is close
Beset with gloom and melancholy till
He feels the half-conclusion which he dare
Not speak, that all is pageantry that seems,
That underneath the surfaces of things
No God of mercy and of love can be
Who cares for aught, save self, and fashions man

The plaything of a day to please his whim,
And then destroys the phantoms of his will,
And like a child at play re-makes the same—
Makes and unmakes nor cares for human pain :—
The mighty heavens in their onward sweep
The chance productions of a tyrant might
Which recks not what they be : the sun may shine,
But he who rules its shining heeds it not :
The stars may twinkle in the depths of night,
But what their purpose is no man can tell :
The earth grows hot and cold, it rains and shines,
And all things grow and wither and decay
And back to dulness creep through Death's wide gate,
Through which the worlds all pass, but no one pang
Of care or sorrow sits upon the brow
Of him who guides the making of the worlds.
Crash rolls on crash and all at last is done,
The end of all at hand, and primal dust
Alone remains with him — a God alone
With ghastly ruins of the lifeless world !
What wonder that the soul of him who kneels,
And seeks a higher than himself in all
The beauty and the glory of the world,
Who asks the meaning of his life, his love,
Who ponders on the mystery of truth,
The grandeur of the human souls he loves.

The holiness of life in all,—should cling
With faith sublime to the great hope that gives
A unity and purpose to all life,
And speak his faith in trumpet tones to all
That Thou, our Father, God, art still in Heaven,
And lovest all Thy works with God-like love,
Eternal, boundless, as Thy boundless life?

BIRTH-DAY THOUGHTS.

God, life, the world, man — spirit, soul, and clay—
O deep mysteriousness of things that change,
And things eternal, changeless, and sublime,
How can we grasp you all and understand
In our short days the wonders that unfold
From world to world through all infinitude!
Have we partaken of the gifts of God,
His freedom, and of all his thirst for good,
And seen his glory and his bounding life,
And felt ourselves the objects of his love—
So deathless, endless, and supreme in all
From age to age and to the outmost bound
Of space and life—that we should be cast down,
And trodden under foot by dark despair,
And held in bondage as the slaves of wrong,
The worshipers of sin, the willing tools
Of evil and of lust, the last, the least,
The only God-forgotten in his world!
Are we alone to think of him with fear,
And walk in trembling in his holy ways,
And if we stumble in the dark, or fall

A prey to weakness, cast ourselves on earth
With agony of soul and deep-bowed face
And beg with broken hearts to be received
Once more into his love! Ah, Father, God,
We do not understand ourselves, nor Thee,
Nor life, nor death, nor sin, nor sorrow's touch
On aching hearts, nor can we fathom aught
The least of all we meet and see, but, oh!
We trust in Thee and walk in simple faith
That all will yet be well. From Thee we came,
And Thou dost know, and did'st foreknow, in all
Thy works their tendency, and what each one
Would do or leave undone in life's great tasks,
And yet of love created'st all to be,
And didst have faith in us that we stamped, God,
In Thine own likeness, loving truth and good,
At length with all Thy creatures would fulfil
Thy will and struggle through the dark and sin
We find around into eternal peace,
Like summer's sun through mists and clouds to noon's
Bright splendor. Man! ah man is Thine own child,
From Thine own life and freedom ushered in
Where he through freedom should his life endow
With graces noble, holy, and divine :
The purest, sweetest, truest, most to be
Like Thee, and most partake of all Thy joys.

And feel himself fast-folded to Thy breast.
Like little children must we all become
In purity, and trust, and truth, and love,—
So said the Christ, the One-Begotten Son,
Our loved, great-hearted Brother, who once spoke,
"O let the little children come to me,
For such are they who enter into Heaven!"

  I know one such, to know her is to know
That God is ever-faithful to his word,
And blesses those with peace who do his will.
May she still feel in every throb of life,
In every joy that comes, in all that meets
Her on her way to him, his great warm heart
With quenchless love aglow encircling close
Her days! oh, may she grow from more to more
In him, and more and more like him, her God.
With angel-songs deep-swelling in her soul,
And gladdening all for her, and making earth
Out-pour its benedictions and its praise
That she was born! May each revolving year
Bestow its richest blessings upon her,
And guide her home, the fragrant "Flower of God,"
While we with ever-thankful hearts confess
Our gratitude to him that he has given
Her life to us to bless us on our ways!

SORROW AND FAITH.

Our human life goes on so full of all
Its mystery and death ; by day and night
Hearts fail and break beneath its load of care
And sin and anguish crushing down to depths
Where spirits lie appalled by suffering,
And feel themselves alone, outcasts of God
And love, and trampled in the dust of death,
And reach in vain in darkness for the hand
Of him who promised evermore to be
The Father of his own, and with them all
In every pulse of life, at every turn,
Upholding, cheering, blessing with his face,
And by his presence sanctifying souls,
And healing hearts disconsolate and sad :
And as they vainly grope to feel the touch
Of that eternal hand laid on their own
Faint in their tribulation, and dismayed
Bow deeper down and ever lower down
In pitiless despair and fearful gloom.
Ah, God ! and is the fault all Thine that we
Lose courage, strength, and faith, forgetting Thee.

Whose life we breathe while thinking Thee afar.
Untouched by what we do or suffer here?
From lips of man in every age the prayer
Goes back to Thee for help and light and life :
Thou heardest their great cry, and sent to them
Thy Son who consecrated pain and in
His lonely agony all-wet with blood
And humbled to the earth showed us that we
Must still be brave and true and trust in Thee.
He cried for pity that the cup might pass,
Three times he cried—and he was Thine own son.
Spotless and pure, sublime in all his ways !—
But still it might not be, and yielding up
His life he prayed at length, "Thy will be done!"
And found the ministering angels near.
He quaffed the chalice to its utmost dregs,
And to the hearts of unbelievers came
The deep deep faith, "This was the Son of God!"
Through victory over self and love for men,
And love for truth and Thee he overcame
The sorrows of the world. Like him must we
In all find Thee who watchest over all,
For not a sparrow falls but Thou dost see.
And are not we the children of thy love?
Man still must trust, and he whose soul is wrung
With deepest sorrows has the largest life

And most partakes of all that is divine.
So he be true.   Send, send to me, my God,
Pain after pain, and sorrow, woe, and grief,
And all the darkness that can fall on life,
And desolation stern as hell can bring.
But keep me true to Thee ; and, oh ! dear God,
—Thou knowest all my hopes, and loves, and fears.—
It sorrows now o'erhang the ones I love.
And I can take and bear them at Thy hand,
Then let them fall on me, nor spare to send.
So they be spared to feel Thee loving still.

A MESSAGE FROM THE SEA.

All-softly moaned the sea with plash on plash
On the long shore with melancholy sound
That spoke its heart-deep secrets to the soul
To hear its voice attuned : the sky was gray
As if with sorrow tinged, and not a leaf
Vibrated to the air, and not a thing
Of life was visible to her who gazed
With mind fast-filled with crowding tho'ts of God
And life and all the mystery of all
The past, the present, and the future days,
Across where sea and sky commingled met
And faded each in each. She watched and watched
As if she waited for the sea to bring
A message from its God and hers to say
That he doth care for all, that not a wave
Can sob upon the shore but comes from him
And writes upon the sand its purest thought,
Its highest wish to live its life in him,
The best its nature can make known to men
Of all his love ; for he does guide the sea
In all its ways, and it in all its moods

Pours forth his praise.   In solitude she stood
With longing in her eyes to hear that voice
Which only can console man's saddened hours
And bring him courage in the gloom that falls
Betimes on every life.   The waves crept in
And died about her feet, their task now done.
Her soul was crowded back upon its walls
And through its walls to him, the Infinite,
And, bursting ever more and more its bounds,
Sank back on God and falling on his breast
Gave all its life to him, as on the shore
The wave its life with gentlest love forsook
And slept in peace its mission at an end.
       To wait and work until the end comes on,
To wait in patience and to work in faith,
In faith deep-rooted in the life of God
And all will yet be peace—So preached the sea.
As wave on wave looked up into her face
And spoke to her of God and fell asleep
Upon the great broad bosom of the world.
She thought of those she loved, for whose dear sake
Her life would gladly perish out of sight
And die to all the world, if so God willed,
That those she loved might ever feel him near
And live with joy in his eternal care.
For them and God her life she would up-yield,

And well God felt the longing of her soul.
And sent her word from every little wave.
"My power still binds the universe in bonds.
And all my power is nothing but my love
Which speaks to thee from all things thou dost see:
O fear me not but trust me all in all.
As I have faith in all that I have made.
Am not I—God—thy Father and thy Friend.
Whose love for thee once yielded up my son.
That thou migh'st know that thou, my child, art mine?
I love thee well with all my heart's great love.
And all of thine are far more all of mine.
Then trust in me and I will bless thee still."
So spake God in the waves. and in the sea,
And in the sands that lay upon the shore.
And in the winds that blew across the world.
And in the heavens that canopied her life.
And she was glad.   The presence of the Lord
Deep in her soul glowed outward in her face.
And there was peace and calmness on her brow.
And strength that comes from consciousness of power.
Of power to conquer all. to trust through all
Her after days the truth and love of God.
To bless him still and pray. "Thy will be done!"

CHRISTMAS GREETINGS.

God's richest gifts be thine this Chtistmas-tide .
His deep eternal love thy life enfold
And all beloved of thee !   May he uphold
Thy days in stately truth : his care abide
With thee, uplifting still to grander height
Thy soul conformed to his, whose gracious birth
To-day anew proclaimed renews on earth
Peace and good-will this holy Christmas night !
I seem to hear the shepherds' wondering speech,
I watch the star that pointed wisdom's way,—
It shines above the child.—My God I pray
By that loved child, his Christ, bless thee and each
To thy heart dear.   A mother's heart must know
The mother-love of God in joy and woe.

THE PILGRIMS.

The earth and all its fulness is from God :
And we are God's, and none must come between
The Father and his child.   The past has been
Too full of woe ; too often man has trod
On God's own spirit full of liberty.
We must anew to all the world proclaim
The holiness of freedom in Christ's name.
And bring to birth a nation, holy, free.
The preachers of the Christ were sent to bless.
As Christ himself did bless, to lead to light
And life in God and not to death and night.
In our new land men freely may profess
Their faith in God, nor must the old-time priest
Destroy the freedom given to men by Christ.

PULPIT ROCK.

(CLARK'S ISLAND)

Within the shadow of the rock I stood
Where on the Sabbath day the Pilgrims prayed
Their hearts' deep prayers : O how the Fatherhood
Of God came to them then, as they obeyed
The distant voice, "My Sabbath sanctify,"
And bowed their heads and hearts and heard the word
They loved, and as the storm swept by
Sang joyful hymns of praise to God their Lord !
And I did think upon those lonely men,
Their sorrows and their hopes, their trust in him,
The One, Eternal God ; how even then
No dark despair their love for him could dim,
And as I heard the echo of their prayer,
I, too, adored our loving Father there.

THE PURITANS.

I

With grateful hearts we think of those brave men
Who loving still their land loved freedom best.
And, loving that, themselves accounted blest
In stress and toil God's freedom to maintain.
In scorn men called them Puritans : the voice
Of God Supreme loud-thundered in their ears
And bade them freedom free, shake off their fears,
And even in tribulation to rejoice.
With giant strokes they fought for liberty
And freed man's mind from man but kept the Book
Wherein God's voice they heard,and read the look
Of Love Eternal's love and the decree
That men are all the offsrping of that love
And subject but to him, their God above.

THE PURITANS.

II

Led by this faith they vindicated God
In his sublimest work and tyranny
Fell down to rise no more.   New England free
Would free the world.   The old-time priestly rod
Was shivered in the high-priest's hand : the doom
Of priestly sway loud-sounded in the earth,
And man, again redeemed, proclaimed his birth
Into the life of God.   To-day the bloom
Of that grand life o'er-arches all mankind
And brightens all the future with its glow :
God's life above is but God's life below—
So felt the Puritan—for God designed
All life and over all his life must reign,
So tyrants fall and freedom bursts her chain.

BISHOP PHILLIPS BROOKS. .

"Father, Thy will, not mine!" It comes to-day
   With saddening sense to all, for he is gone.
   The mighty-hearted lover of Thy Son,
Our "other Christ," who taught us how to pray.
The noble-hearted bishop is at rest:
   At rest on earth, but still he lives in Thee,
   His Father, Lover, Friend, while sadly we
In deepest pain confess, "Thy will is best!"
Man's noblest man in all this later age,
   The preacher, prophet, Christ-man is gone home:
   Thy call he heard. "My well-beloved, come!"
In Thee he lives. Our grief we must assuage
   And live like him for Thee till we shall meet
   Our God-like bishop at the Master's feet.

BISHOP PHILLIPS BROOKS

I opened all the windows of my soul,
Flung wide its doors and let the light stream in
That came through him from God. In me no sin
Could then abide : no waywardness control
My thoughts, or words, or deeds. God's Spirit moved
Most mightily my life through his great life—
Himself controlled by Christ, who mid the strife
And questionings prevailed, and dying proved
The mightiness of love.

            A man indeed
Was he Christ-hearted in his ways ! So true !
Forgetful of himself God's image grew
In him to richest bloom. The Master's creed
In him triumphant lived, and still in death
He makes me throb with his undying faith.

FATE.

The spirit is fled
That had quickened his body now lying there dead.
And the white weeping moon
From the high-vaulted sky
Looks down in her paleness as hurriedly by
She darts as though fearing a moment to stay
And longing to hasten the dawning of day
That now cannot come oversoon.

In the calm twilight.
Ere the earth went to rest or the stars to beam bright.
A youth trod all alone
Over loneliest ways
With a sad look of pain in his eyes' weary gaze.
And a face in its ghastliness lovely to see,
As though flying quick from the cruel decree
Of a Fate that pursued him unknown.

No kind one he met
With pitying word or with heartfelt regret
To lighten his pain,
But with eager wan face

He hurriedly sped as if seeking some place
Where peace might at last reach his overstrung soul,
Or Fate its evangel of pardon unrol
And a message of mercy might deign.

How vainly he fled!
He's now lying dead in his blood all so red
And his pain all is gone :
There is no one to weep
O'er his beautiful corpse as it lies there asleep
And frightens the moon who speeds on in her flight
To hide fast from her eyes that heart-killing sight
By hurrying onward the dawn.

TRUTH.

I am no tyrant.   I stand and watch
The destinies of worlds and men.   The tyrants
Fear me and try to kill : or failing this,
To mask my face that men may know me not :
And error for a time with narrow minds prevails.
But God is Truth, and men are God's and mine,
And I at length must win, so fear me not.

GOD'S BOOK.

Holy is life, God's gracious gift to us
From his own life sublime : no narrow wish
To live self-centred rules the heart of God :
But he, out-pouring from his love on men
Compels by love that they should love in turn.
From him came life and love, and back to him
Our love and life must go. He restless longs
For us : our passing years are his alone :
In them we write his wondrous history
Page after page, a far diviner work
Than that of prophet or evangelist.
Their pages die, but thine, God's child, will live
Immortal as thy God. Write, write thy best !
The worlds will pass and they are Nature's leaves
Writ by Omnipotence, but thou canst write
Upon the pure white leaves of thy young soul
A book of God-enduring peace and love
And stamped and sealed by the Eternal's hand.

www.ingramcontent.com/pod-product-compliance
Lightning Source LLC
Chambersburg PA
CBHW030005030726
47499CB00008B/2899